SHIFTING MAGICK TRILOGY

LIA DAVIS

Shifting Magick Trilogy
By: Lia Davis

Published by After Glows
© 2015 Lia Davis

eBook ISBN: 978-0-9964303-0-2
Paperback ISBN: 978-0-9964303-1-9

Interior format by The Killion Group
http://thekilliongroupinc.com

All characters in this book are fiction and figments of the author's imagination.

www.AuthorLiaDavis.com

DEDICATION

*To Mr. Davis with all my hear*t

OTHER BOOKS BY LIA DAVIS

Paranormals

Ashwood Falls Series
Winter Eve
A Tiger's Claim
A Mating Dance
Surrendering to the Alpha
A Rebel's Heart
Divided Loyalties
Touch of Desire
A Leopard's Path
Jaguar's Judgment

Ashwood World
An Alpha's Fate

Bears of Blackrock
Bear Essentials
Bear Magick

Sons of War Series

War's Passion
Ashes of War
Artemis's Hunt

Shifting Magick Trilogy
Moon Curse
Moon Kissed
Moon Mated

Vampire Lords
It's A Vampire Christmas

Contemporaries
Pleasures of the Heart Series
Business Pleasures

Single Titles
His Guarded Heart

MOON CURSE
BOOK I

Moon Curse

Olivia Kelly is cursed. The eldest of three witches, she is doomed to spend her existence alone unless she finds and mates with a male descendant of the moon goddess, Artemis. Just when she thinks that all hope is lost, a handsome - and very naked - Alpha wolf stumbles into her life.

Sawyer Scott has been spelled to turn into a house cat once a month during the full moon. A humiliating predicament for an Alpha, and one that has kept him from his Pack every full moon for the last year as he searched for the witch responsible. In a last ditch effort to find the crazy old lady; he stumbles upon a scent he can't deny. His mate.

CHAPTER ONE

Bottle of wine. *Check.*

Two boxes of tissue. *Check.*

Sappy-cry-your-eyes-out chick flick. *Check, check.*

Another Friday night with no flowers, no hot guy pampering her, and no friends to help her feel sorry for herself. Correction. No *single* friends to feel sorry *with* her. Of course, her non-single friends had asked her to come hang out with them. *No, thanks.* She wasn't in the mood to watch the happy lovebirds enjoy each other's company while she pretended not to notice.

It'd only add to the heavy weight on her heart and mood. It didn't seem right to call her sisters, either. Ever since their grandmother had told them about the Kelly curse, they'd made it their mission to find out a way to break it. A task that had become too emotionally draining. She didn't have the energy for it. The curse would be there tomorrow and the next day.

Each of their curses was different, but they all involved mating. Audrey, the middle sister, had to mate someone who'd been kissed by a god. Diana, the youngest, had to mate with her true half before midnight on her thirty-third birthday.

Olivia's curse was to find a man who was a descendant of Artemis, goddess of the moon and the hunt. Olivia had no idea where was she supposed to find this demi-god. She'd already tried consulting a time traveler and got laughed at.

Whatever. She didn't need a man. Living alone allowed her to do whatever the fuck she wanted. Besides, there weren't many guys who liked a short, curvy woman over age thirty-five. No, they liked them thin and young. Not to mention, she came from a family of crazy witches.

Settling into the corner of the sofa with a glass of wine in one hand and the boxes of tissues within reach, she clicked the play button on the DVD remote. "Ahh, the joys of being a cursed, mateless witch. I'm so pathetic."

About ten minutes into the movie, she heard scratching at her back door followed by a soft meow. Glancing around the room, she spotted Midnight, one of her two black cats, sleeping in the window near the front door. Sam was nowhere to be seen.

With a heavy sigh, she sat her glass on the end table, pushed *pause* and stood. "How the hell does that cat get out?"

She padded through the kitchen to the rear entrance. When she opened it, she frowned. It wasn't Sam; it was an orange tabby. The poor thing looked hungry and cold.

When she scooped the cat up, it hissed and growled at her. "Now, that is uncalled for."

As if her voice calmed the little beast, it stopped its verbal protesting and peered up at her with gorgeous gold eyes. A quick peek under its tail told her that the cat was a male. He slapped at her, and she *tssked*. "Behave. I had to check to see if I needed to lock you up separate from my boys, but since you're not female, you should be fine."

"Are you hungry?" She opened the cabinet and pulled out a can of cat food and a saucer.

After setting the cat on the floor at her feet, she opened the can and dumped the contents onto the plate. She then placed it on the floor in front of him, but he didn't want it. Olivia shrugged. "That's all I have, bud."

Picky-ass cat. As she re-entered the living room, the phone rang. *Now what?*

"Hello."

"Oh. You're home."

Olivia rolled her eyes at her grandmother's cheerful tone. "Where else would I be, Grams?"

There was a brief pause before her grandmother spoke again, making Olivia suspicious about what the crazy old witch had been up to. She loved Grams like a second mother and would do anything for the woman. However, Grams wasn't all there at times. At the age of four hundred fifty years old, she was the oldest witch alive.

"I wanted to see if you needed company. There is a new spell I want to show you."

Olivia rolled her eyes. Even through the phone she could tell Grams was lying. But why? "No, Grams. I was just about to go to bed. I had a long day at the shop."

The shop was called Kelly's Enchantments and was the family-owned magick and gift shop. It really had been a busy day, and every day that week, people had come in wanting either the recipe for a love spell or for Olivia or one of her sisters to make one for them.

Each of the Kelly sisters refused, and each time, the customers would get annoyed. Some even got angry.

Humans just didn't understand that the Universe had a sense of humor at times. Besides, it was very literal about granting blessings. It was never a good idea to simply ask for a man to love. Because the type of man that entered your life may or may not be the ideal one. No, specific details were needed to properly grant the heart's desires.

"Ah, yes. The love spells. Just give them colored sugar water and send them on their way." There was a hint of a smile behind Grams' dry tone.

Shaking her head, Olivia held in a laugh. "Why did you call again, Grams?"

It wasn't that Olivia didn't like talking to her, but the older witch got distracted easily. If Olivia didn't stir Grams back to the main subject, they'd be on the phone all night.

"Oh, yeah. I saw a wild beast run into your yard a few minutes ago. Do be careful about taking in strays."

Olivia drew her brows together. What was she talking about? "No wild animals here. Besides, I have a protection spell on the house."

"Good. Good. Just be careful. You never know what you allow into your home." Grams paused for a brief moment, then continued. "I have to go feed the cats."

There was a click, and the line went dead.

That was odd. Then again, it was Grams. Most of what she said or did never made sense.

After setting the phone on the end table, she clicked the *play* button on the remote and sank into the corner of the sofa a little more.

Not even two minutes later, a loud crash sounded from the kitchen. She jumped to her feet, causing the remote to fall to the floor, and turned in time to see a large, naked man standing in the archway between the living room and kitchen. Her heart hammered and panic rose, restricting some of her airflow. Yet she couldn't tear her gaze from his perfectly sculpted body.

"How...how did you get in here?"

He didn't speak, just bored those gorgeous gold eyes into her as he stepped forward. Her body shook and she darted to her right to grab her broom. Midnight hissed and fled out of the room.

Coward.

Holding up the broom like a batter at home plate, she glared at the man. "Don't come any closer."

One side of his sensual lips lifted as he continued his slow prowl toward her. Her body warmed at the sight of his broad shoulders rolling with each step. Dropping her gaze, she flushed and snapped her attention back to his face. Good grief, he was huge, everywhere. She had a strange, naked man in her house pinning her with his gorgeous gold eyes and she was ogling him like a double fudge sundae. Damn, she was going insane.

She swung the broom before darting to the other side of the room, effectively putting space between them. "Don't make me hurt you."

A bitter laugh escaped him and his eyes darkened. "You can't hurt me."

Arrogant ass. She took another swing at him, only to have him catch the broom in one hand and jerk it from her grasp. Knocked off balance, she cried out when he caught her, wrapping his strong arms around her waist.

Heat flooded through her, overwhelming her senses and stealing her ability to think. *What the hell?*

She struggled then groaned as he tightened his hold, pulling her back against his front.

His hard length pressed into her back, drawing a groan from her. Desire ran hot in her veins. "How did you get in my house?"

He buried his nose in her neck and inhaled. She squeezed her eyes shut, trying like hell to ignore her body's reaction to him. Confusion clouded her thoughts. He was a stranger for crying out loud.

"You let me in." His husky voice was soft with a slight crack as if he too were fighting off a wave of desire.

What? She didn't let him in... Her grandmother's words about the wild beast and not letting in strays entered her mind. *Damn. Grams, what did you do?*

CHAPTER TWO

Sawyer ground his molars together. His cock throbbed while his senses filled with the female's scent.

Mine.

His wolf growled the single word as he paced under Sawyer's skin.

A soft curse slipped from her lips as she stilled. "You were the orange cat."

"I'm cursed. I need your help to break it."

Her scent soured a moment before she brought one bare foot down on his hard enough that he loosened his hold on her. Squirming out of his arms, she fled to the kitchen. With a low growl, he followed.

When he rounded the corner, he froze. The female held a large knife in one hand and had a cell phone to her ear with the other. "You really don't expect that knife to keep me from you, do you?"

"Stay back," she rushed out, then said, "No, not you, Grams. Tell me more about the wild beast you saw earlier."

He cocked his head but couldn't make out what the other person on the phone was saying.

After a few yeses and an uh-huh or two, she hung up the phone and glared at him. "How did you get cursed?"

"I was minding my own business, hunting actually, and some crazy witch threw some kind of powder at me and started speaking in a language I didn't recognize. The following full moon, I shifted into that damned orange cat." He thrust a hand into his hair in frustration. He couldn't go back to his Pack until the full moon cycle was over. How could he face them?

The Alpha of a wolf pack who shifts into a house cat upon the full moon... Yeah. He'd be challenged for his Alpha status for sure.

"The witch isn't crazy." The female moved to the sink and lowered the knife. She frowned then shook her head. "She's old. And forgetful. And...a little nuts at times. But that doesn't give you the right to call her crazy."

"You know the witch?"

Her shoulders dropped and she turned to meet his stare. "She's my grandmother."

"Then you can fix this."

"I'm afraid not. I don't know what she used in the powder, or how she invoked it, let alone why she did it." She raised the phone and studied it for several moments before she laid it and the knife on the counter.

When she moved past him, he gripped her arm. Heat swirled around his hand and traveled up his arm. "Where are you going?"

She pursed her lips and narrowed her eyes. "To get a few of my spell books."

With a quick jerk, she freed her arm and pushed past him toward the hallway. He fell in step behind her. "How long will it take to break this curse?"

She whirled around, coming within inches of him. "It isn't a curse. It's a spell. There's a huge difference."

A bitter laugh escaped him before he snarled. "Turning into a house cat for three fucking days is definitely a curse."

His harsh tone didn't faze her. She jammed her index finger into his chest. "One, don't growl at me. Two, the more you badger me, the longer it will take to figure this out."

When she pivoted away from him, his gaze lowered to her ass while his lips twitched. The wolf within pawed at him to move closer and bite. "What's your name?"

She spun back around and her gaze narrowed as she studied him before answering. "Olivia."

She turned once again and moved down the hallway. Stopping about mid-way, she muttered something too low for even his wolf hearing to pick up. A moment later, the ceiling opened and a wooden ladder formed. Without a word, she climbed the ladder and disappeared into the hole.

Not knowing what the hell the witch was doing, he followed her. He emerged inside a large attic bathed in candlelight. In the center was a large white circle. When he moved closer, he noticed it wasn't drawn in paint but salt.

"What's that for? Summoning demons?"

She took a deep breath and exhaled loudly as if annoyed by his question. "Don't touch the outline."

Glancing at her, he froze. She'd gathered her long, thick brown hair up in a messy bun and wore a pair of reading glasses. Couldn't witches create a spell to fix vision impairments? As if sensing his internal question, she lifted her lashes over the glasses that rested on the end of her nose.

"I don't have a vision impairment. These are spelled to help me read the Book of

Shadows." She returned her attention to the book on the podium.

Curious, he moved closer to her. Her cinnamon apple scent wrapped around him, drugging him. He leaned in and inhaled. His wolf howled in his head, and the man agreed. This female was theirs.

"Are you sniffing me?" Irritation leaked out with the words she spoke, but she didn't look at him.

Straightening, he stepped away and scanned the room. Bookshelves lined the wall next to them and the one behind Olivia. A few feet away sat a large oak desk with opened books and papers scattered across its surface. His need for order urged him to straighten the papers. At least put then in a neat stack.

"Don't touch my desk, wolf."

He cut her a narrowed gaze, not surprised that she knew what he was. She was a witch, a very powerful one that could apparently read his thoughts. "It's Sawyer. How do you know what I'm thinking?"

"I'm very good at reading body language." Her words were soft, but the slight way her scent sharpened told him she was lying, or at least omitting something.

He let it go because it wasn't uncommon for mates to hear each other's thoughts. But that usually happened after they'd bonded. Was it possible for them to connect without the mating because she was a witch?

Focusing on her, he sent her a thought. *What are you looking for, my mate?*

Her hands stilled on the book and she lifted her head. "I'm trying to figure out which spell my crazy grandmother placed on you. *And*, I'm not your mate."

His lips tugged into a lazy smile. Closing the distance, he cupped her face. "If you weren't my mate, then you wouldn't have heard me."

She shook her head but didn't speak. The scent of her arousal drifted around him, drawing a growl from deep within his chest. Slipping his hand to her nape, he pressed his lips to hers. A groan escaped her and she opened for him, meeting his tongue half way. Raw sensual need rushed through his veins with each caress of her tongue against his.

Tearing his mouth from hers, he growled. "I need you...now."

"Yes," she said, breathlessly. Her blue eyes brightened, and tiny pricks of white light flashed across her irises.

He removed her glasses, gently laying them on the podium, and then walked her backward until her back flattened against the wall. Her curvy body fit perfectly against his. A groan left her, pleading. His dick jerked at the sound, and he captured her mouth once more, sucking on her bottom lip before dipping his tongue inside. She tasted of wine and berries.

Damn.

Fisting her nightgown, he gathered the cotton up her thighs then stepped back enough to jerk it over her head. Her large, round breasts rose and fell with each breath she took. Her rosy nipples hardened under his stare.

Raw sensual hunger raced in his veins, and he dipped his head to tease one nipple with his tongue. Olivia inhaled sharply then let out a low moan. Dizzy with the desire to possess her, he cupped her, slipping his fingers through her moist folds.

"You're not wearing underwear," he growled.

Her response was breathless. "I...I was in my night clothes."

"Naughty girl," He whispered into her ear before nipping her lobe.

A shudder went through her and she fisted his hair, pulling until their gazes met. Silver swirled inside the blue depths of her eyes. Then her skin took on a slight glow, like she was lit up from the inside. It made him wonder how powerful of a witch she was.

When he opened his mouth to speak, she tugged his head to hers and kissed him while wrapping her legs around his waist. Out of reflex, he thrust inside her and hissed through his teeth. Then froze as she inhaled sharply. *Damn it.*

"You were a virgin." He drew back to stare into her watery gaze. "I hurt you. I'm so sorry."

When he started to pull out, she locked her legs behind him. "Don't. Make it feel good, please."

She ran her nails up his chest, stopping to circle one of his nipples. Tingles skittered over his skin. When she rotated her hips, he groaned then buried his nose in her neck. In smooth strokes, he moved in and out, slowly at first, then faster as the pleasure built.

Her nails scored his shoulder blades as she pressed her head to the wall, her soft moans turning to cries of pleasure. His balls tightened, but he held back, not wanting to fall over the edge without her.

"Come for me, my witch," he whispered.

As if waiting for the command, she screamed out as her pussy squeezed around him and her body shuddered. Only then did he let go and tumble into his own release.

Panting, he stepped back, taking her with him. He wrapped his arms around her. "Sorry."

She nipped his shoulder with her blunt teeth. "It's my fault. Besides, that was incredible."

He frowned. "And you are basing that on what experience?"

She pressed her hands against his chest and wiggled her way out of his grasp. Once she was on her feet, she picked up her nightgown and disappeared into the small bathroom a few feet away. Through the closed door, she said, "I wasn't a virgin."

Bullshit. He yanked the door open. "I don't believe you."

She rolled her eyes before sliding the gown on. "It was a one-night stand in high school. My first broken heart. Happy now?"

"No." He glared at her. "I kind of wish I was your first. You are *my* mate."

She pushed by him. "And you are spelled to turn into a cat at the full moon."

His lips twitched as he watched her curvy hips sway while she made her way back to the podium. She had a fire he craved in a partner and the strength his Pack needed in an Alpha's mate.

CHAPTER THREE

Oh, gods. What was wrong with her? She'd just had sex with a total stranger in her spell room. The fact that Sawyer was her magickal mate didn't excuse her lack of control over her hormones. However, the impulse to do something reckless, and the desire the large and intense wolf stirred in her were too strong. Stronger than any love spell she had ever encountered.

She froze. Love spell?

Damn.

She conjured her phone and dialed her grandmother. The older woman answered on the third ring. "Yes, dear."

"You cursed a wolf to turn into a cat during the full moon. What spell did you use?" Olivia rushed out.

Silence filtered over the connection briefly before Grams spoke. "No, no...he wasn't supposed to turn into a cat. The damned beast ran off before I could finish."

Olivia took deep breaths, trying to calm her mounting anxiety. What she really wanted to do was scream, and possibly choke her grandmother. *She means well, Liv.*

In a calm, soft tone, Olivia asked, "Grams, do you remember what you used in the spell?"

"It's his own fault. If he had only stayed to let me finish... Where is he now? Did you see him?" Grams' voice cracked slightly as if she were confused.

Glancing over at Sawyer, Olivia frowned. The man glared at her with his arms folded. A mix of annoyance and desire swirled in his gold eyes. "Yes, he's here."

"Really? Well, then." Grams paused, and the sound of paper being shuffled came over the phone. "That's odd. I don't remember this one."

"One what?"

"Oh, dear."

Olivia was a second away from marching the two blocks to her grandmother's house and taking all of the woman's spells away. "What. Did. You. Do?"

Sawyer closed the distance between them and let out a lower growl. Olivia pressed a hand to his chest and nearly groaned at the hot, raw power he possessed.

"Liv, hon, don't growl at me. The spell can be broken by true love's kiss."

Seriously? Were they living in a fairy tale? "No, Grams, that didn't work."

Her grandmother laughed. "It has to. Try again."

Then there was silence.

"Grams?" Fuck. The woman had hung up on her. What the hell did she mean true love's kiss? Sawyer was truly Olivia's mate, and they had done more than kiss moments ago. Her body heated at the flashes of memory.

"Call her back. Make her give you a straight answer."

Olivia snapped her gaze to Sawyer and glared. "There is no reasoning with her. She's old and gets confused."

He crossed his large, muscular arms over his bare chest. Olivia groaned, recalling that Sawyer had no clothes. No wonder it was hard for her to focus. She snapped her fingers, conjuring a pair of sweatpants and threw them at him. "Put those on."

One dark brow rose as his lips twitched. "I'm perfectly comfortable in the buff."

"I find it hard to focus. If you want me to reverse the spell, cover yourself."

A light chuckle escaped him, but he put on the sweats. "What did your grandmother mean by a kiss?"

"A whole lot of nothing, obviously. She's been obsessed with fairy tales for the last year." Olivia forced her attention back to the Book of Shadows—a book of spells, recipes, and rituals passed down through her family for over four hundred years.

"Kiss me again."

Not looking at him, she shook her head. "We may be mates, but we aren't in love. We just met. That has to be what went wrong."

He stepped closer and she stilled. Heat coiled around her as she breathed in his rich earthy scent. Good gods, the wolf stirred a desire from deep inside her. She didn't even know a need that raw existed.

He leaned into her, pressed his lips to her ear, and said, "What if I bite you and make you mine?"

Glancing at him and studying him for several long moments, she let his words sink in. That was it. True love's kiss for a wolf is the mating bite. Could it be so simple? Not that mating a wolf was an easy task.

"I think that is exactly what Grams had in mind."

Sawyer stared into Olivia's dark blue eyes, not sure he had heard her correctly. "You agree to be my mate to break the curse?"

She held up a hand. "Not so fast, wolfman. I'm just saying the mating bite could break the spell. I know nothing about you or where you came from."

He looped an arm around her waist and pulled her to him. "There will be plenty of time to get to know each other. You are my mate, and I know you feel it, too."

"I'm not sure what I feel. You confuse me." She averted her gaze.

Cupping her chin, he lifted her beautiful blue eyes back to his. "Wolves mate for life. Once we find our other half, there is no other as long as she lives. I'm the Alpha of Gold Ridge."

Her eyes widened slightly. "The Alpha?"

He gave a short nod. "I have been for the last forty years. I have one brother, who is one of my sentinels. I've been searching for you for so long."

"I still know nothing about you. Does your Pack like you?"

"What kind of question is that?"

She shrugged and pushed out of his arms. "I don't want to be stuck with an Alpha who isn't good to his people. There are some cruel people out there, especially those in powerful positions."

In one smooth but quick movement, he lifted her hand and pressed her palm to his chest. "Use your magic to see my soul. I know you can do it because we are mates."

She pursed her lips but did what he asked. After closing her eyes, she relaxed her shoulders. A moment later, warmth traveled from her hand to inside him, winding around his heart before branching out to race through him. It wasn't uncomfortable. It was calming to his wolf, which in turn, calmed the man.

When she opened her eyes and removed her hand, his wolf whimpered at the loss of contact with its mate. Olivia tilted her head slightly then rose on her toes to press her lips to his. "I can't fight fate. But what if mating doesn't reverse the spell?"

He caressed her cheek with his knuckles. "I don't want you to do this for me. I can't force you into something you don't want."

"One thing you must know about me is that I never do anything I don't want to." Her perfect, kissable lips lifted in a smile, which faded a moment later. "Grams isn't supposed

to practice magic alone. I'll have to see why
one of my sisters wasn't there."

"Maybe Grams turned them into frogs."

Olivia slapped at him playfully. "Not
funny."

He let his smile turn serious. "I'm not
laughing. I can't go back to the den as a cat."

"Well then, let's see if we can break this
spell." There was a hesitation in her tone.

With one brow raised, he studied her for a
long moment before speaking. "You're going
to mate me?"

She rolled her eyes. "Hello, Mr,
Romantic." She held his stare and poked a
finger into his chest. "I have conditions."

"What kind of conditions?" His lips
twitched.

"First, don't expect me to move into your
den right away. Second, I'm not to be bossed
around. And third, I'm free to live my life as I
choose." She raised her brows in challenge.

He let out a growl as he gripped her hand
and lifted it to his mouth. "You are free to be
you and continue your life as you please. As
far as bossing you around, there is only one
person an Alpha answers to. That's his mate."
He kissed her knuckles, sending a rush of heat
straight to her core. "You *will* move into the
den with me, but I'll give you until the next

full moon to come to me on your own. If you don't, I'll hunt you down."

CHAPTER FOUR

Oh, gods. The promise in his words amped her desire. Could she truly find the peaceful life she craved with him? She'd finally have what she wanted. A mate. Someone to share intimate thoughts and dreams with. Someone to break her own curse.

"A witch's bond is forever, too. Even after death on many occasions. It is not something I would give freely." She turned away, not wanting him to see the emotions building inside her. Not wanting him to know the truth behind her decision not to fight the mating urge.

His body heat enveloped her as he closed the small gap between them. Her own body hummed in anticipation, knowing what the Alpha wolf could do, and had done. Squeezing her eyes shut, she tried to clear her thoughts but it was next to impossible.

"You are hiding something from me."

She sighed and dropped her shoulders. It was no use lying to him. Once he bit her and began the mating bond, both their minds would open up to one another. Their darkest secrets, deepest desires, and most treasured thoughts would be revealed. After all, that was the point of the bond. To become one in body, mind, and soul. To love unconditionally as it was fated from birth.

"I am also cursed." He stilled with his hands on her shoulders. "All the daughters in my family are in one way or another. My youngest sister, Diana, must mate before her thirty-third birthday or she will become undesirable to everyone outside her family. Audrey, the middle sister, can only mate a male kissed by one of the gods. We're not even sure what that means."

A warm tear rolled down her cheek. *Damn it, Liv, you are stronger than this.*

"What about you?"

She was doomed to be unhappy for the rest of her short existence. Taking a deep breath, she turned to stare into his gold eyes. "I can only fall in love with a man who is a descendant of Artemis, goddess of the moon and the hunt."

His brows dipped, but one side of his mouth twitched. A sense of hope drifted from him. She wondered if he knew something about her curse. Before she could ask, he said, "I'm the eldest son of the fourth-generation descendant of the moon goddess."

Shock froze her in place. How could it be? He would have to be…well, old. Thoughts of his encounter with Grams and the spell she had placed on him churned in her mind. Had her grandmother known who he was? Had she known that Sawyer could be the one to break her curse?

Olivia didn't care. For the first time since learning of the curse on her and her sisters, she felt hopeful for her future. The fact that she felt the mating pull toward Sawyer was a bonus.

A low growl rumbled from him as he stalked closer. Her heart hammered, and for an instant, she thought to run. No. She wouldn't run from him. A wash of awareness fell over her. He was her mate. Her one true mate.

She wanted this. Wanted him. Curse be damned. "What if we can't bond?"

"Then we'll deal with it. Leaving you now that I found you is not an option." He scooped her up, drawing a squeak from her.

"Where are you taking me?"

"Somewhere more comfortable. I'm not fucking you up against the wall again."

Well, then. She giggled, not able to stop herself. Opening her mind, she visualized that they were on her bed, then allowed the magic to pull them there through the astral plane.

When they appeared in her bed, Sawyer raised one dark brow at her. She shrugged. "I have many talents."

"I look forward to exploring them all." He kissed her nose, then her lips.

When he dipped his hand between her thighs and cupped her, she sucked in a breath at how tender she still was from the sex upstairs.

"We can't do this. Not now."

Panic rose within her. "What? Why?"

She'd dreamt of the day she'd find her demi-god and break the curse, and he was going to deny her?

He pressed a finger to her lips. "Calm down, love. We can form a mating bond without sex. In fact, since we just made love, it isn't a problem at all."

"Oh." She relaxed a little.

A brilliant smile formed on his strong, handsome face. "Olivia, my mate, I promise to honor you and do everything in my power to allow our love to grow to unbreakable lengths for as long as we both live."

"Love?"

One side of his mouth lifted, widening his smile even more. "My wolf and I already know we're in love. We knew the moment we caught your scent."

Her heart swelled. "I feel…" Oh hell, who was she fooling. The moment he walked into her living room, naked, she somehow knew, as well. Her mother had always said love is strange and wild. If her heart fluttered just looking at him, then she was in love.

"I think I'm in love, too. I accept you as my mate and will honor your love for the rest of our long, long lives."

He struck hard and fast. A sharp sting of pain erupted but was quickly replaced with overwhelming pleasure as his fangs sank into her skin. Oh, gods. His Alpha power mingled with her witch's magick, twining around each other until they merged into one.

A moment later, she felt him inside her mind, body, and soul. Her curse was broken.

Tears rolled down her cheeks. *Thank you, goddess.*

CHAPTER FIVE

The room filled with magick, making the hairs on Sawyer's nape and arms stand on end. Both moon magick and his Alpha power swirled around them. Fuck, it felt too damn good to take her as his mate.

The strings of their mating wound together in a magickal dance, forever linking them as one. The heavy magick slowly disappeared as he removed his fangs and held her, their hearts beating in sync with the other. Their bond was strong. It was one of the signs of a true mating. Not that he'd had any doubts after he'd caught her scent.

"I think I'll stay here for the month I'm giving you to decide to move into the den." He kissed her temple.

She let out a soft laugh. "The bond is much more intense than I thought it would be."

"It's a strong union."

She fell silent for a moment then lifted to hover above him. "Get dressed. I want to see if the spell on you is broken."

When she darted away and off the bed, he caught a glimpse of sadness in her eyes. His chest tightened. Had her curse not broken? No. He refused to believe that. It had to have.

After rising from the bed, he followed her through the house and out the back door. At first he hesitated, unsure. Manning up, he stepped out under the moonlight and waited.

Relief flooded him when he didn't turn into an orange house cat. He glanced at Olivia, who stood a few feet away staring at him. A small smile lit up her face. Her blue eyes glowed, then rippled like a wave under the moon.

Suddenly, her eyes filled and she held her hands out to him. Instantly, he went to her. He would give her anything she desired. Stopping inches from her, he took her hands in his. "What's wrong?"

Her bottom lips trembled slightly. "I feel you in my heart. It's like we are soul mates, brought together after a long time apart."

"It's wonderful," he agreed before kissing her. She sighed and melted into him. His mate. There was no way he'd be able to share her with the Pack. The mating was too new. "I think we need to stay here at least a few more days, just the two of us, before I take you to the den. I'm not ready to share you with them yet."

She locked gazes with him, a small smile tugging at her lips. "Sounds good to me."

"What? No comment about being selfish?"

She shrugged. "I'm feeling a little selfish myself." She stood on her toes and kissed him soft and quick. "I'm newly in love, and I want to bask in the glow for a little longer."

Overjoyed at hearing the words from her, he picked her up. "Anything my mate wants, she gets."

"Anything?"

He threw his head back and laughed. "Within reason, yes."

"I guess that goes both ways."

Yes, it did. "I love you."

Her face lit up and the silver returned to her blue eyes. "I love you, too. Always."

The End

MOON KISSED
BOOK 2

Moon Kissed

Audrey Kelly has given up. As the middle sister, she is required to mate with a male kissed by the gods in order to break her part of the Kelly curse. An impossible task, even for a witch. However, when her older sister mates with a descendant of the moon goddess, Audrey's hope is renewed. Her new brother-in-law claims that his brother could be the one to break Audrey's curse. But could Lucian really be her one true mate?

Sentinel leader, Lucian Scott has no desire to find a mate. He's content with his single life. Or so he thought until a curvy, little witch comes into it. The mating urge slams into him almost immediately, and his need to possess Audrey in every way possible makes it unbearable to stay away from her. Too bad his brother, the Alpha, has given him a direct order to do just that. Keeping his distance until the so-called time is right may just be the death of him, but Audrey is definitely worth the wait.

CHAPTER ONE

Apparently, when an Alpha mates, it's a big fucking deal.

With a sigh, Audrey traced the rim of her wine glass as she sat at a small table closest to the large, two-story brick house her older sister had moved into last month—after mating to an Alpha wolf the same night she'd met him. Olivia was insane. She had to be.

Then again, Audrey's sister had found her one true mate and broken her curse. Sorrow seeped into Audrey, amplifying her already grumpy mood. It wasn't that she was unhappy for Olivia. Finding a mate and breaking the curse placed on her from birth was wonderful. Amazing. Not to mention, Olivia looked like she'd won the lottery, ten times over.

As she should. Olivia was so head over heels in love she glowed from it. Plus, the curse that hung over her head, similar to

Audrey's, had been broken. Her Alpha mate was a descendant of the moon goddess. In fact, he was a first generation shifter. Just the man to break the curse and give Olivia everything she desired.

Audrey glanced to the happy couple slowly dancing in the middle of the Pack circle. Her heart ached. Unlike Olivia's curse, Audrey's mate had to be kissed by a god. The prophecy was so vague she didn't even know where to start looking.

So, she'd given up years ago.

Apparently, she was doomed to be alone, mateless, and childless for the rest of her existence. A lump formed in her throat, but she pushed it away. She didn't need a man or children in her life.

"Pennies for your thoughts."

The low rumble of the male's tone rippled through her, stirring things long dead. She lifted her lashes and met the heated stare and beautiful gold eyes of Lucian Scott, the Gold Ridge Pack Beta, Sentinel leader, and her sister's new brother-in-law.

The wolf was right out of her dreams, the perfect male. Lean muscles covered his tall frame. His dark brown hair fell just below his ears, framing a handsome face with a shade of beard. He'd unnerved her the moment they met hours ago.

Picking up her drink, she downed the last swallow and hoped he would leave. The last thing she needed was a gorgeous wolf making her crave things she'd never be able to have.

When he sat in the chair next to her, she rolled her eyes. "Have a seat."

He leaned into her, draping an arm over the back of her chair and growled, "I will."

Cocky SOB. Need raced through her like a wildfire, heating every part of her body. Good gods, this wasn't happening. Knocking her arousal down a few notches, she scooted several inches away from him. "What do you want?"

A rumble sounded from his chest, not quite a growl. "Do you really want the answer?"

Yes, please. No. She didn't. She couldn't, even for a moment, entertain the idea... What was she talking about? He was sex poured into the perfect male body. And she'd had just enough alcohol to not give a shit.

Plus, she was cursed to never find her mate. So, what would it hurt to have a little fun for once? To be wild and have mind-blowing sex with the wolf next to her. Facing him, she smiled. "Yes, I would like to know your answer."

The corners of his sensual mouth lifted, stirring to life a desire she'd never felt before. "I want to take you somewhere private, strip you bare, and lick every inch of your perfect, curvy body."

Well then. Ask and you shall receive. It suddenly became hot, and it had nothing to do with the alcohol. She reached out and fingered a button on his black dress shirt. "Then what?"

"You are a naughty little witch."

"One, I've never been little. Two, you don't even know how naughty I can be."

Who the hell was that woman who'd spoken?

Abruptly, he stood. Gripping her hand and pulling her with him, he stalked down a small path away from the party. She glanced over her shoulder to see her sisters watching, both with wild smiles.

Great. They'd badger her in the morning for details.

Her strawberry scent intoxicated him. Her curvy, perfect body begged for his hands. The need to possess her in every way possible turned into a raw hunger he'd never experienced before. In fact, until he saw her he'd never considered taking a mate. His loyalty was to his brother—his Alpha—and making sure their enemies couldn't get near him. Lucian didn't have time for a mate.

His wolf thought otherwise, and what the wolf wanted, the wolf would get.

Lucian tried to ignore the pull toward the beautiful, curvy witch for the four hours she'd been in the den. A battle he'd lost to the wolf currently pacing just under the surface. Glancing at her profile as they walked away from his brother's mating celebration, he watched how the soft lights from the lanterns strung around the circle kissed her creamy skin. Her shoulder-length black hair framed her round face perfectly. When she turned to him, his cock hardened and he lost himself in her green gaze.

She averted her eyes instantly, but not before he noted the slight color in her cheeks. Her scent sharpened, indicating she too was aroused.

"It's a nice night out," she said softly.

He moved closer to her so his hand brushed against hers. "Yes, it is."

What was he doing? Acting like a nervous juvenile.

He linked his fingers with Audrey's and tugged her to a stop. Looking into her green eyes, he cupped her head and claimed her mouth. She tasted of wine and berries. When she opened and tangled her tongue with his, he lost what little control he had left.

Walking her backwards, deeper into the forest, he gathered her long skirt up to her hips. She groaned and pressed her breasts against him, intensifying the desire running hot in his veins. He slipped his hand between her thighs and growled at how damp her panties were.

"So wet," he whispered in her ear.

"Yes."

Brushing the cotton aside, he slid two fingers through her folds. She gasped, then moaned as she moved her hips against him. He entered her and pumped his fingers in and out while rubbing her clit with his thumb. She gripped his arms, her nails biting into his biceps. Soft moans turned into pants right before she shuddered in release.

Just as he unbuttoned his jeans, he caught his brother's scent. Lucian pressed his head to Audrey's and lowered her skirt. "My brother is looking for us."

Dazed, she stared at him for a moment, then blinked. "Oh."

Pushing away from him, she adjusted her clothes. When Sawyer came into sight, Audrey darted away. Most likely heading back to the Pack circle.

"Sawyer," Lucian growled, not bothering to hide his annoyance.

"Diana isn't feeling well and needs a ride home," Sawyer spoke loud enough for Audrey to hear him as she fled to where her sisters waited.

Setting his jaw, Lucian held his brother's stare while he waited for Audrey to get out of earshot. Irritation clouded his thoughts. Why had his brother interfered? After a long moment of holding the Alpha's narrowed-eyed stare, Lucian lowered his shoulders. "She's my mate."

"I know."

"Then why did you stop me?"

Sawyer raised one broad shoulder. "You can't claim her yet. It has to be under the Hunter's Moon."

Confusion clouded Lucian's mind, and he began to think Sawyer was losing his. "What are you talking about?"

"It's part of her curse. At least it is what Olivia believes. You can't claim her until the full moon." Sawyer turned and disappeared into the trees.

What the hell was his brother talking about? "Sawyer!"

"I mean it. Don't mate with her until the full moon."

Fuck. Sawyer was a stubborn ass. His tone in the last statement told Lucian he wasn't getting any more answers. The Hunter's Moon was two weeks away.

Lucian would go mad waiting that long to see his mate again. On second thought, Sawyer hadn't said not to seduce the curvy minx.

CHAPTER TWO

Audrey's body hummed from the orgasm Lucian had given her moments ago. Her legs felt like jelly and she didn't know how long she'd be able to stand there while her older sister talked them into staying. She didn't know if she should be mad at, or grateful to Sawyer for showing up when he had. By the gleam in the Alpha's gaze, he'd most likely scented both hers and Lucian's desire.

Good mother of the moon. She hadn't ever felt a need so raw and intense before. Lucian Scott made her ache all over. That was why she needed to leave the den.

"Stay the night," Olivia's cheerful voice rang in her mind, cutting through the storm of thoughts.

Audrey shook her head and opened her mouth to tell her sister no way, but Diana spoke up first. "That would be great. Wouldn't it, Audrey?"

"Yeah, sure. Just great." Audrey tried not to grumble the words. The Alpha had lied about Diana not feeling well. His actual motive for interrupting her and Lucian was unclear.

Just then, Sawyer stepped behind his mate and wrapped his arms around her. The glow on Olivia's face stirred a new ache in Audrey. Heartache. Audrey averted her gaze, only to have it land on Lucian. The male had a crooked smirk on his sensual lips as his heated stare held hers.

"We could have breakfast together," Lucian said, his eyes never leaving hers.

Olivia looped an arm with Audrey's, drawing her in close. "Yes, that would be great. A whole family breakfast."

Audrey didn't bother stopping her smile. For the first time since they were children, they had a family. Of course, they'd always had Grams, who was a little nuts but a wonderful mother figure.

Stepping out of her sister's hold, Audrey faked a yawn. "Can you show me to my room? It's been an exciting and exhausting day."

"Of course." Olivia linked her fingers with Audrey's, then Diana's and tugged them toward the house.

Once inside, Olivia crossed her arms. "Spill."

"What?" Audrey tried to shield her emotions from her sisters, but they knew something was up. Being the oldest, Olivia had the mom face down to an art. Releasing a breath, Audrey frowned. "Lucian is impossible."

Diana giggled, drawing Audrey's attention. "It's not funny. The wolf is so...so large, and..."

"Hot," Diana added on another laugh. "I don't see what your problem is. Go after him. Enjoy yourself."

Audrey had planned to do just that until the walls around her heart had fractured once the wolf's lips touched hers. She couldn't get attached to him with the curse hanging over her head. He may be a descendant of a god, but that didn't mean one had kissed him.

If she slept with him and the curse didn't break, Audrey would lose herself to him and never be able to bond with him. A constant emptiness would form in her soul, forever hungry for something she couldn't have.

No, she had to stay away from the male.

It was three in the morning, and Audrey couldn't sleep. She was in a strange bed—alone—and in a strange house. The energy flow she was accustomed to wasn't right. It wasn't like it was in her own place. Here, it was too primal and made her skin crawl.

She blamed a certain wolf for it all.

Thoughts of Lucian tumbled over and over in her mind. His scent clung to her, even after the hot shower she'd taken moments ago. Damn him.

Giving up the fight with sleep, she flung the covers off and stood. The house was quiet as she made her way down the hall and out the back door. She didn't bother changing out of her nightgown. One, it was a comfortably warm spring night. Two, everyone was asleep.

She inhaled the calming scents of night jasmine mixed with the clean mountain air. Conjuring a steaming cup of tea, she sat on the swing and stared out into the dark forest. It was peaceful there, as long as she ignored the surge of energy created by Lucian. Why in

Hades had she let the wolf invade her mind and body?

A rustling sound came from a few yards away, making her sit up straighter and scan the area. She didn't have night vision like the wolves, but she could see better than a human. Especially when she opened her third sight. However, she didn't need her extra witch senses to know who was out there.

Lucian. She sagged into the wicker patio chair and wished he'd go back where he'd come from. "Couldn't sleep?"

His deep chuckle vibrated through her like a sensual touch. "Not with you in the den."

Ugh. "You could be a little more subtle."

"You know as well as I do what's going on."

Did she? Not really. Yes, she was attracted to the large, gorgeous male. She also knew enough about shifters to know that Lucian had started the mating dance. As much as she'd love to join the dance and play with the wolf and the man, she couldn't bear the heartache it would cause in the end.

There would be an end.

"I'm cursed. I can never complete the mating with you."

He was crouched in front of her within seconds, taking the cup from her and sitting it on the deck beside her chair. A surge of power bounced between them when he linked his fingers with hers. "You will never know unless you take the chance."

"I'm too tired." She broke the connection and pushed at him so she could stand. He rose with her but didn't let go of her. Narrowing her eyes, she stared into his gold depths. "Your brother says you are descendants of the moon goddess. Have you met her?"

One corner of his full lips lifted. "I have met Artemis a few times."

Her pulse increased slightly and hope bloomed in her chest. *Have you been kissed by her?* The question churned in her thoughts and rolled on her tongue, yet she couldn't ask him. The fear he'd say no was too crippling.

She flattened her hand on his chest and pushed. Tears stung the back of her eyes and her nose started to tingle. "I have to go."

When she turned her back, he wrapped his arms around her and held her body to his. His warm breath brushed against her cheek as he answered her thoughts—a sign of being true mates. "I've been kissed by more than one goddess."

She froze in place. It couldn't be so easy. Turning in his arms, she met his stare. Words failed her as she scanned his features. He could break her curse. Why did she feel that something else was missing?

"Take a chance, Audrey. You are my mate. I feel it growing stronger by the minute. Not even the Fates are that cruel. Besides, if I weren't, I wouldn't have been able to hear your thought. Your plea."

She squeezed her eyes shut and nodded. His soft, commanding lips came down on hers in a hungry rush. Heat flooded her veins and she couldn't deny him. It'd been too long. Lucian felt... right.

He tightened his hold on her, crushing their bodies together. Breaking the kiss, he rested his forehead against hers. "We should go to my place."

"Yes. Before we wake everyone up."

Desire lit up his eyes, making his gold irises glow as he took her hand and led her to his cabin a few yards away. All the while, she tried to control the rush of heat spreading up her arm. Her heart beat rapidly, and she was sure he heard it with his super-animal hearing.

Calm down. You're acting like a teen at the prom. If only her prom date had looked like Lucian. The wolf was lean, yet muscular with a dust of a beard. Rough and gorgeous rolled into a sexy as hell alpha male.

And he was hers for the taking.

Suddenly, a wave of unease flowed across her skin. She smashed the feeling before it took root. Lucian was right, the only way to find out was to just let go and get over her fears of being forever alone.

They came to a stop at his front door, and he faced her, one brow raised. "Are you okay?"

"Yes." The way he pressed his lips together before opening the door told her he didn't believe her. *Damn wolf senses.*

Once inside with the door shut, she whirled around, coming face-to-face with him, she cupped his cheek and kissed him. Like the one in the forest earlier that night, it was hot and threatened to overload her senses.

Hot, raw desire rushed through her veins, heating her everywhere all at once. When he drew her body flush with his, the wildfire sparked to life, consuming her until all she wanted was the male in her arms.

The ache between her legs begged for him as their tongues danced and their mouths glided over each other. She moaned and squeezed her thighs together.

He tore his mouth from hers, his breaths coming in short draws as his wolf peered at her from his golden depths. Damn, he was hot.

"I'm too impatient for foreplay," she burst out.

His lips twitched. "Good." It came out on a growl that vibrated through her.

Much too fast for her to track, he jerked her nightgown over her head and tossed it to the floor. On instinct, she covered her curves, only to have him grip her wrists and spread her arms out to her sides. "Don't hide from me, ever. You are perfect." He kissed her forehead. "Every beautiful, curvy inch of you."

Her heart melted. She'd never had a problem with her weight, and his admission melted away the small amount of insecurity she felt. A sense of flirtation rose within her and she crinkled her nose at him. "Then take me."

Walking her backwards until her knees touched the arm of the sofa, he undid his jeans and freed his cock from its confinement. Good gods, he was beautiful, in a manly kind of way.

"My eyes are up here," he teased, drawing a laugh from her.

"Yeah?"

Instead of responding, he stepped between her thighs and wrapped one arm around her while lifting one of her legs. Dipping his head, he teased a nipple. She gasped and let her head drop back. Tingles raced over her skin and her pussy throbbed, wanting him inside of her.

As if knowing what she was thinking, or needing, he thrust inside, stretching her. Pleasure slowly built as he pumped his hips, sliding in and out. He felt too good, too right. She scored his back with her nails and rode the wave of raw energy mounting between them. It was unlike anything she'd ever experienced with any of her other lovers. Magick swirled, connecting them in a way that renewed her hope to break the curse.

He increased his thrusts, burying himself deep inside of her. Her moans turned into cries of pleasure until she thought she'd explode from desire. Then he struck. The sting of his fangs piercing her shoulder made her gasp. The pain quickly shifted to pleasure and came in a rush of bliss as an orgasm crashed into her.

Lucian's body tensed, then convulsed as he met his release, as well. She hugged him and rested her forehead against his shoulder. Nothing had changed. Wasn't the bite supposed to start the mating? If so, she couldn't feel him inside her like Olivia had described.

After a moment of awkward silence, Lucian pulled out, then with an index finger lifted her chin. "What is it?"

"The curse didn't break." A lump formed in her throat as she spoke the words out loud.

"Are you sure?"

Was she? Gods, she was confused. "Nothing's changed."

"Sometimes it takes time for the mating to take hold. It's different from couple to couple." His gold eyes told her he believed what he said.

She wasn't sure she did. Sure, she trusted him. Her witch senses would tell her if he lied. However, there was obviously something she'd missed in the wording of the curse. "I...I have to go." She grabbed her clothes and pushed past him while tugging her nightgown down as she ran out the door.

Her chest tightened as tears blurred her vision. Never again would she believe she'd ever be happily mated. That was why she needed to get—and stay—far away from Lucian.

CHAPTER THREE

Lucian paced his living room. Not seeing Audrey for the past two weeks had driven him mad. Nothing he did eased the edge his wolf was on. All because he'd promised his sister-in-law he'd wait until the full moon.

The night Audrey walked out of his house, he'd chased her until Sawyer reined him in using his Alpha power. Brother or not, Lucian couldn't go against a direct order of the Alpha. No amount of arguing had convinced Sawyer or Olivia to allow Lucian to go to his mate.

"Lucian," Olivia's soft voice drifted from the open door of her and Sawyer's home. When he didn't reply, she stepped out onto the porch and tapped the toe of her shoe. "She's hurting and has stopped talking to me."

He glanced over his shoulder and his irritation melted a little. Olivia hugged her middle, and her eyes were red as if she were crying. Damn it. Taking a deep breath, he reined in his wolf before speaking. "She's hurting because we are mates. The more time we spend apart, the worse it will get."

"I thought the curse would have kept her from feeling the mating." Olivia lifted her lashes, a mix of hope and regret in her blue depths. "That makes me wonder if the curse indeed broke when you two…"

Her cheeks colored and she averted her gaze.

Turning to face her, he held out a hand. She stared at it for several moments before she took it. Lucian gave it a gentle squeeze, a sign of trust because he knew of her telepathic ability. "If that is true, then she hasn't fully accepted me as her mate."

"She's scared."

He nodded and kissed his sister-in-law on the cheek. "I plan to seduce her into believing."

Audrey blew out the candle and rocked back on her heels, her eyes closed and her breathing slow and steady. The lingering magick from the full moon ritual charged the air around her and kissed her skin. Focusing, she gathered the energy to her and directed it into the earth beneath her bare feet, grounding and centering herself at the same time.

Opening her eyes, she smiled at the renewed energy. The last two weeks had been restless. Her skin felt too tight and her heart hurt. It was that wolf's fault. Damn him for stirring desire in her. When she'd run away, he hadn't even chased her.

A sign that he wasn't her fated mate despite what he'd claimed.

Absently, she touched the small bite mark on her shoulder. The mark meant for a mate. Why hadn't the bond formed? She knew why, but didn't want to think about it. Lucian had made his choice by not hunting her down like a mate should have.

After cleaning up her ritual items from her outdoor altar, she carried everything into the house. Jazz, her smoke-grey cat meowed at her as she entered the kitchen. "You can't go out."

She kicked the door shut with her foot, only it didn't click closed. Glancing over her shoulder, fear burned in her belly as she dropped the wooden box of ritual items. The top of the box broke off when it hit the ground, and the contents scattered over the tiled kitchen floor. Poor Jazz scattered from the room.

"Damn it, wolf, what the hell?" She bent down to clean up the mess.

"Sorry. I thought you heard me." He squatted with her and reached out, but she slapped his hands away before he could touch any of the items. The last thing she needed was for his energy to transfer to her ritual tools.

"No." Annoyance mixed with embarrassment fluttered inside her. "Why are you here?"

"To see you." He cupped her chin, drawing her attention to his face. Gold eyes watched her so intensely her body warmed.

No, she couldn't get attached to him. The curse prevented her from mating with anyone except *the one*, and she was beginning to believe he didn't exist. However, she was a woman and had needs. She wouldn't turn the sexy wolf from her bed. A weakness that would break her heart over and over again.

"Why?"

He paused and stared at her. "Why what?"

"Why are you here to see me?"

He moved closer to her as she set the box on the table beside them. "You're my mate."

Oh, no. This was so not fair. "No I'm not. You need to leave."

There was no way in hell she'd get her hopes up, only to be crushed like a bug hitting a windshield. Again. She stepped forward and pushed him toward the back door. Once her hands touched his skin, wild energy flowed from him up her arm. Suddenly, his primal, sage scent filled her senses.

He snaked an arm around her waist, jerking her body to his. "You feel it. The need is alive; wild, and raw. My wolf calls to you."

Yes, she felt it. And damn, she wanted it more than the air she breathed. Yet, it hadn't worked the first time. Why would it be different the second time? "Why didn't you chase me then?"

He tugged her into a hug and cradled her to him. "Olivia believed that it had to do with the full moon, plus, you needed space. She had Sawyer order me not to go after you until now."

Lifting her head, she gazed into his face. His features were a combination of worry, hope, and stress. The dark circles under his eyes indicated he hadn't slept much. Join the club. She hadn't slept either. Every time she closed her eyes, he was there. Sexy and alluring.

"What if it doesn't work?"

"Open your heart to me and my wolf and it'll happen. If not, we'll keep trying until the Fates give up their games. I know in my soul you are my mate. I can't rest until I have you by my side." He cupped her cheek and kissed her softly on the lips.

Breaking the kiss, he drew back to stare at her. "You do want to mate with me, right?"

She slapped at his chest. "Yes. It hurt that you didn't chase me. I mean, at the time I didn't want you to. Olivia was right that I wanted some space, but at the same time I kept expecting you to show up. When you didn't…"

Her chest tightened again. Before she could twist out of his embrace, he hugged her closer. "Never think that I don't want you. It killed me, and on several occasions I almost disobeyed a direct order from my Alpha."

The sadness she'd felt over the weeks melted into regret at being angry with him. No matter how much he wanted to, he couldn't go against a direct order without abandoning his Pack. She knew that much about Pack life from Olivia.

"Hey," Lucian whispered and lifted her chin. "Even though she wanted me to wait, your sister now thinks the curse might have broken already, just not as obviously as it did with her."

Frowning, Audrey searched through her thoughts and emotions she'd gone through since meeting Lucian. The flood of intense desire when he was near, his electrifying touch, and the longing when he wasn't there were all signs of finding a mate. All signs she'd ignored because she was afraid to open her heart.

Hope bloomed in her belly and spread through her. Could Olivia be right about the curse?

Lucian stepped closer and caressed her cheek. "You're thinking too much. Follow your heart and just let it happen."

Follow her heart…

Every time she and her sisters discussed the curses in front of their grandmother, the old woman would ramble on about true love and how it conquered all.

"Not even the darkest of curses can stand in the way of true love. Once the heart opens, love spills out and purifies the soul," Grams rattled off while Audrey and her sisters rolled

their eyes and continued to look through the
Book of Shadows.

The memory dissolved, replaced by
Lucian's handsomely concerned face. The
words Grams had spoken so many times sank
in. "Stupid. I knew the answer all along.
Grams had told us almost every day of our
lives."

"Told you what?" Lucian's brows bunched.

Audrey laughed and shook her head.
"Sorry. My crazy grandmother had said
nothing could stand between us and true love.
An open heart is a pure heart. I thought she
was just rattling off craziness. Hell, we all
did."

"I've met your grandmother. I could see
why you would think that."

She cut him a narrowed-eyed glare, and he
laughed and pulled her into his arms. She
cupped his face and lowered the walls around
her heart. He was her mate. "I've been so
afraid, confused, and wrapped up in trying to
break the curse that I never saw what was in
front of me."

She stood on her toes and pressed her lips
to his. Warmth spread from everywhere he
touched her, seeping into her skin and making
her hypersensitive to him and the wolf within.
The magick he possessed in his soul that

married him to his animal half called to her. She opened her senses and allowed her own magick free.

Iridescent waves of energy flowed around them and through them as their mouths moved against each other and their tongues tangled. She broke the kiss and stared into his gold eyes. A sudden knowledge snapped into place and her heart swelled. "I want to be with you for the rest of our existence. Curse be damned. I'm falling in love with you already, and have been since first seeing you two weeks ago at the den. We're Fated to be together and I don't want to fight it."

A spark lit up inside her and she gasped as awareness like nothing she'd experienced before spread through her. Lucian's emotions flowed into her like a lifeline.

Lucian dipped his head and kissed her lips lightly. "It's the mating bond."

Glee bubbled up. "I accepted it." Tears spilled over her eyes. "We're mated."

He wiped the tears away with his thumb before he scooped her up and walked toward her bedroom. "I love you, Audrey Kelly, with all of me. Forever."

"I love you, too." She kissed him as he laid her on the bed.

A wicked grin formed on Lucian's lips. "First thing in the morning, we'll pack up your things and move you to the den."

"Anything you wish, my mate."

EPILOGUE

Two months later

"So, are you going to spill the reason why you are practically glowing joy?" Audrey was ready to burst. If her sister didn't tell everyone of her news, she wouldn't be responsible for her actions and would spill everything.

Olivia glanced across the yard to where Terrence, one of Sawyer's Sentinels, walked toward them, an annoyed gleam in his eye. Behind him was a determined Diana.

Lucian laughed, his chest rumbling into Audrey's back. "Looks like a witch chasing a wolf."

"Yes. Diana can be persistent." Audrey giggled.

Sawyer nodded. "I see that. You two leave her alone. It'd do Terrence some good to be chased."

When the couple reached them, Diana glanced from Audrey to Olivia. "What's up?"

"Have a seat." Olivia gestured to the patio chair next to her.

Sawyer gave Terrence a nod, which Audrey took as a request to stay because the wolf crossed his arms and stood on the opposite side of the group from Diana. Interesting.

Olivia cleared her throat. Once everyone turned to her, she said. "I'm pregnant."

A rain of congrats and a few howls from the wolves surrounded them. Lucian nipped Audrey on her ear before whispering, "When can we share our news?"

"Later. When I'm past the first trimester." She was thrilled to be a mother, but didn't want to share the news just yet. So much could happen in the first few months. However, with the wolves' sensitive noses, she couldn't wait much past the third month. She had two more months to keep it between just Lucian and her.

"I suck at secrets, you know."

"Yeah, but you'll keep this one."

He raised a brow. "How are you so sure?"

She kissed him. "Because, you hold on to the same fears I do. Plus, you like keeping this to ourselves."

"The only thing left to do is get your baby sister mated before her birthday next month."

Audrey smiled and glanced at Diana. "I think she's already working on it."

"Ah, yes. It will be fun to watch Terrence run."

Yes, it would. Audrey just hoped the wolf didn't run for long. Lucian hugged her tight. "Don't worry, we'll give him a little push or a kick in the ass if he doesn't come to his senses soon."

"I have the best mate."

He kissed her temple. "So do I."

The End

MOON MATED
BOOK 3

Moon Mated

Diana Kelly is the baby of three witches and, like her sisters, cursed. She must find her one true mate before midnight on her thirty-third birthday or risk becoming undesirable to everyone outside of her family. With her sisters happily mated and curse-free, Diana holds on to hope for a miracle. However, the clock is ticking, and she's running out of time, and options.

Terrence Miles is a lone wolf, loyal only to his Alpha. When he meets the youngest Kelly sister, he's mesmerized by her beauty and soft curves. His wolf pushes him to claim her, but the man is hesitant. He's never imagined himself mated. Could their mating break her curse and satisfy something in him he didn't know was missing?

CHAPTER ONE

"What do you mean, you helped?" Dread sliced through Diana's gut as she stared at her grandmother. *Please don't say you weaved a spell.*

The elder witch had been banned from stirring potions and casting charms. One, her memory wasn't what it used to be. Two, she, like all the rest of the Kelly witches, was cursed. Grams had never found her true mate to break the spell. Although she'd married and deeply loved Diana's grandfather, the curse was never broken.

Grams' curse had become a reality when Papa passed away a month after Diana's mother was born. She'd never found anyone else to spend her long life with. As a result, Grams grew lonely and had gone a little...well, crazy.

"Grams," Diana prompted, tapping her foot on the tile floor of her kitchen.

Grams rolled her eyes then opened the fridge. Her long, silver hair fell over her shoulder when she bent to open the veggie tray. "I just cast a small spell to help that stubborn wolf of yours see what's in front of him."

Oh, gods. Diana's stomach soured. "Did you use those exact words?"

Grams stilled briefly before closing the fridge and facing her. "No, no. Silly girl. I used your name."

Patience wasn't something Diana had ever mastered. But getting angry with her grandmother, who usually didn't make sense, wouldn't make the situation any easier. The last spell Grams had cast was a love spell to "help" Olivia find her true mate. Technically, it did help, but the spell was wrong. Grams had turned the Alpha wolf of Gold Ridge into an orange house cat.

Fear gripped Diana's heart at the thought of what kind of spell Grams had conjured up to aid in her search. Especially since Diana had indeed found her mate, or at least believed she had. *Damn it*.

"Grams, do you have the spell written down? Can you give it to me?"

Grams bobbed her head. "Of course, I wrote it down."

Closing her eyes, Diana took deep, calming breaths while visions of a den full of wolves transforming into cats popped into her mind. "Do you have it on you?"

"No." Grams closed the fridge then said, "You're out of eggs."

Seriously? "I'll get them when I go to the store next week."

"No, no, I'll get them." Grams pushed by her and left. A moment later, her car pealed out of the driveway.

"She doesn't need to be driving, either," Diana muttered and grabbed her cell.

Olivia picked up on the second ring. "Hi."

"Hi. How are things there?"

"Great, why?"

Diana dropped her shoulders, thankful her sister couldn't see her. "No reason. I was going to stop by in a little bit. You up for company?"

"That would be great. I'll call Audrey, and we'll make it a little party." Olivia's excited tone flowed from the other end of the call.

Smiling, Diana pushed away some of her panic. "Great. I'll be there shortly.

"See you soon."

Diana ended the call with a sigh. She needed to make a stop before going to her sister's. The last thing she wanted to do was face Terrence, but she wouldn't be able to relax thinking that Grams had done something to him.

Thanks, Grams. They should really look into a nursing home for senile old witches.

Diana wiped her clammy hands on her jeans and tried to soothe the huge knot in her belly. She needed to calm down. The man behind the door she stood in front of was only a person. Well, he was more than that. He was a sexy-as-hell wolf shifter that made her ache all over.

It wasn't like her to shy away from others. She had no problem talking with strangers and telling them what was on her mind. However, when it came to the quiet, lethal wolf behind the door, she fumbled over her words and her heart beat erratically.

Gathering her courage, she knocked and waited. How pissed would he be if she left before he could answer the door? *Stop it, Diana, you're being a child.* She was thirty-two for crying out loud.

A wave of sadness fell over her, and she wrapped her arms around her waist. Her birthday was less than a day away. She'd been unsuccessful in getting Terrence to claim her before time ran out. Once the clock struck midnight on her thirty-third birthday, she'd become undesirable to everyone but her family. She would forever be alone, never to be a mother or know the loving touch of a mate.

The door opened and she lifted her blurry gaze to Terrence Miles, one of Sawyer's—her new brother-in-law and Alpha of Gold Ridge—Sentinels. His piercing brown eyes narrowed, showing a soft hint of concern. "What's wrong?"

Shaking her head, Diana averted her gaze. "Nothing. I…I thought I'd stop by on my way to Olivia's."

Terrence folded his arms over his broad, bare chest. His nostrils flared slightly, indicating he was scenting her for a lie. "Why?"

The single word came out as a growl. Her body warmed at the sound. By the way Terrence thinned his lips, she guessed he'd caught the change in her scent. Damn.

"As I mentioned, I'm heading over to Olivia and Sawyer's. I thought you might want to come with." It was the only thing she could think of to say in order to avoid telling him that her crazy grandmother had been playing with magick again.

After a long moment—and a raised eyebrow—he stepped back and disappeared inside his home. A moment later, he reappeared with a tight black T-shirt stretched across his broad chest. Shit, he was hot. Her skin heated, and her heart pounded as he stepped onto the porch, invaded her personal space, and shut the door. She swore she heard him inhale slowly before he moved away and descended the stairs.

Closing her eyes, she tried to slow her heart rate and push away the desire. Yet, she couldn't. The last thing she needed was to get attached to him before her curse took effect and turned her into an undesirable hag. Mate or not, Terrence had made it clear he wasn't interested when they'd first met.

With less than twenty-four hours left, she didn't have the energy to try and change his mind. After all, there was a chance the curse wouldn't break. Then he'd be stuck with her. No, she couldn't—wouldn't—do that to him or anyone. Even if that meant she'd turn crazy like Grams.

She straightened her spine and followed Terrence down the dirt path leading toward the center of the den and Olivia and Sawyer's house.

About halfway there, one of the enforcers stopped Terrence to discuss security or something. Diana wasn't paying too much attention as she stepped around them to continue on to her sister's home. Then the male talking with Terrence spoke, stopping her in her tracks.

"It's a pleasant surprise to see you, Diana."

She whirled around, eyes wide and a spark of dread flaring within. The thought that Grams' twisted magick spell was at play entered her mind. *Okay, you're being silly and paranoid.* "Thank you, I think."

The male smiled widely. His light blue-gray eyes lit up. He was handsome, but her heart didn't pound wildly like it did with Terrence. "If you're not busy, I'd like to show you around the den. It's a beautiful day for a walk."

Oh no, Grams. What did you do? None of the males in the den had paid any attention to her in the past. Before she could reply, Terrence stepped between them and let out a growl. "She's busy."

Terrence gripped her arm in a firm but gentle hold and tugged her toward the Alpha's home. Diana let out a giggle and tried not to break out in a full laugh. All humor left her after three more males stopped to talk with her and give her gifts. Each time, Terrence seemingly grew more and more jealous, growling and threatening each one with the loss of body parts.

Crap. This wasn't good.

CHAPTER TWO

In his five hundred plus years, Terrence had never felt jealousy so intense. He wanted to kill each male who offered Diana gifts and promises of a good time in the short walk to Sawyer's place. Raw, primal need to claim the female raced through his veins. His wolf wanted to mark her so everyone would know whom she belonged to.

Wait. No, he didn't want to mate. His life was as he wanted it. Alone, and free to protect his Alpha at all cost. Mates complicated things.

When Sawyer opened the door to the house, Diana rushed by Terrence and Sawyer. The sharp scent of her anxiety filled Terrence's senses. "Olivia!"

Diana's sister entered the room, brows dipped in concern. "What's wrong?"

"Grams. She did it again. Why can't she just leave things alone?"

Huh? Confused, Terrence watched Olivia wrap an arm around Diana and lead her to the sofa. "Calm down and explain what you mean."

With a deep, shaky breath, Diana closed her eyes briefly before speaking. "Grams said she helped me. I tried to get her to explain how and the spell she used, but you know how confused she gets. Anyway, that's why I really wanted to come over. I stopped off at Terrence's to see…" Diana met his gaze briefly before giving her attention back to her sister. "Well, to see if he was a cat or something."

Terrence laughed. "I can ensure you that your grandmother hasn't been here."

Diana shook her head. "She doesn't need physical contact."

Olivia sighed. "Why are you so upset?"

"Because I was approached by four males on the way here who all want to court me."

"Oh," Olivia said and stood. She held out her arms, and a large, leather-bound book appeared in her hands. "Sounds like an attraction spell. Or it could be another love spell. We never know with Grams."

Terrence stiffened. While he understood why the crazy old woman would cast a spell, he didn't like the sound of a love spell. Especially if it worked on everyone but him. Unless he was already in love...

Studying Diana, sitting on the sofa with her arms wrapped around her waist, he took in her natural beauty. Her perfect curves and round face were just two of the features he'd noticed when he'd first met her. He'd never denied the attraction he had for her, he just wasn't interested in mating anyone. Or so he kept telling himself.

He crossed the room and sat next to her, taking one of her hands in his. She tried to pull it away, but he tightened his grip. "I'm not affected by the spell."

Her lavender eyes lifted to meet his. "Why not?"

"Because you are his mate," Sawyer's voice boomed through the living room as the male entered from the hallway.

Terrence growled at his Alpha while Diana jerked out of his hold and moved out of reach. "Stay out of my head, Alpha."

Sawyer chuckled. "I don't have telepathy, nor do I need it to know. You've been distracted since meeting her. Now, it sounds like if you don't claim her, someone else will."

Jumping to his feet, Terrence stalked toward Sawyer. "No one claims her."

Sawyer raised a brow and crossed his arms over his chest. "Then mark her."

Terrence glanced over his shoulder. Diana shook her head then pointed at him. "No you don't. One, I will never know if it's not Grams' spell. Two, I'm cursed to turn into a hag at midnight."

"You're not going to turn into a hag," Olivia stated calmly. "Plus, mating your true half will break the curse. It may break Grams', too."

"We don't know that for sure." Diana inched closer to the door. "I need to think."

She turned and ran out the door, letting it slam behind her.

Terrence ignored his wolf's demands to chase the curvy witch down. He needed answers first. "I used to think I didn't want a mate. I don't need the complications."

Olivia huffed. "Complications?"

Glancing from her to Sawyer, Terrence opened his mouth but no words came to him. He was a loner. Always had been. The only reason he'd stayed in Gold Ridge was because

Sawyer had asked him to, and Terrence owed the Alpha a debt.

Sawyer clasped him on the shoulder. "You may believe your own bullshit, but I don't. Denying your wolf his mate can be very painful. I haven't had to use my power over you in the years we've known each. Don't make me do it now."

His mate? Diana?

The room fell silent, all eyes on him, making his skin itch. "Diana isn't my mate."

Olivia let out a breath and rubbed her round belly as if soothing the child she carried. "Diana has given up finding her mate. I'm afraid she'll lock herself up—both physically and emotionally—after tomorrow."

Dread jabbed him in the gut. The sorrow in Olivia's voice stabbed him in the heart. "What are you not saying?"

"When a witch falls into a depression, she can either go insane, or literally will herself to die." Sawyer hugged Olivia.

Diana's smiling face flashed in Terrence's mind. From the few times he'd seen her in the den, he'd always found her fascinating. She was so full of light. However, when he'd spoken to her earlier, he'd realized that light had dimmed.

Oh hell. "What's her address?"

Olivia rattled it off with hope in her tone. He feared she would be disappointed when he came back, unsuccessful in breaking Diana's curse. Without another word, he exited the house and gazed into the sky. "Goddess, I could use a little help. Or a sign of some kind to tell me what the hell I'm supposed to do."

CHAPTER THREE

Diana sat with her legs folded like a pretzel and her eyes closed in the middle of her back yard. She inhaled slowly and released the breath after a moment while calling to the element of air. Her magickal element. The one thing no one, not even the gods, could take from her.

The slight breeze picked up and swirled around her, spreading its fingers through her hair and kissing her skin. Being so in tune with the air, she could connect to everything that used it. She sighed and opened her eyes at the sounds of butterfly wings.

A flutter of color floated around her. A few of the butterflies landed on her knees and in her hair. She let out a breathy laugh. "It looks like it's just you and me, guys."

Her heart ached a little more. There was no way she'd be able to see her sisters in their perfect, happy lives. Wow, that sounded bitter. *Suck it up. I will not feel sorry for myself. Period.*

She was a witch. That wouldn't change. Magick ran in her blood, and she could perform illusion spells in her sleep. She'd spent her adult life perfecting the craft, preparing for the possibility that she may not find a mate to break the spell.

It was settled, then. She didn't need a man, or a certain wolf Sentinel that could melt her panties off by staring into her eyes.

Great, she'd never get the damned wolf out of her head. He would haunt her dreams for the rest of her long life.

With a flick of her wrist, the butterflies scattered and then disappeared. She rose to her feet and stilled at the sudden shift in the air. Terrence's sensual sandalwood scent enveloped her. Crap. What the hell did the male want?

"What did you do that for? Where did they go?"

She turned at his words and narrowed her gaze. "Who?"

"The butterflies."

"Oh. Umm, I sent them on their way because I was about to go inside." Unable to meet his intense stare any longer, she gave him her back. "What do you want?"

"You."

"Only because my crazy grandmother cast a spell."

"I said before, I'm not affected by it."

She refused to turn to look at him because if she did, she'd weaken. The pull to him was stronger than before. Most likely because there were only a few hours left until her thirty-third birthday. Midnight marked the time when the curse would force her into a life of solitude. "How do I know that for sure?"

The sound of leaves crunching under his steps made her breath hitch. She squeezed her eyes shut. His scent enveloped her, alluring and pure male. What would one last fling hurt? Besides her heart. A moment later, Terrence wrapped his arms around her and his breath brushed against her neck as he spoke. "We'll have to take that chance. You are my mate, I just didn't know how much I wanted it until those other males approached you at the den."

"Why? I mean, the wolf would have known before either of us. Not unless the man just ignored all the signals. From what I hear, when a wolf finds his mate, the beast won't rest until he has her." She sagged into him a little more. Defeat rolled through her. What would it hurt to take a leap, find out if they were truly fated to be together? "If the curse doesn't break, you must leave before morning."

He nipped at her earlobe. Tingles raced over her skin before settling inside her belly. His low voice caused goose bumps to erupt on her skin. "To answer your question, I ignored my wolf. I can be a very stubborn male. Plus, I believed I was better off alone and content with protecting my Alpha. I was a lone wolf before coming to Gold Ridge, and thought I'd grow old that way. As for leaving you, that will only happen if the mating doesn't take. Even then, I'm not sure I could walk away."

Her heart thumped rapidly. Was he really her mate? She turned in his arms and stared into his dark gaze. A sensation more like a knowing filled her. "I don't want to hope for something that might not happen. I'm tired of hoping, tired of chasing a dream."

He ran his thumb over her bottom lip. "Don't think. Just let me pleasure you tonight."

Heat flooded her body, making it impossible to refuse him. She didn't want to. That *should* scare her. If there were even a small chance of breaking the curse, she was going to take it. Her heart be damned.

Threading her fingers into his shoulder-length hair, she tugged his head down and claimed his lips. Instantly, he tightened his hold on her, crushing her body to his and deepening the kiss.

A moan escaped her as a hunger she'd never known rocked her. Her worries melted away until it was only the two of them in that moment.

He walked her backwards and through the door of her screened-in patio. Diana ached for him to touch her just as he slid his hands to her ass, squeezed and then gathered the skirt of her dress up.

She sucked in a breath when he cupped her over her dampened panties. Passion uncurled in her, making it impossible not to beg him to take her, hard. His warm fingers brushed the thin cotton aside to sink through her lips.

Digging her nails into his shoulders, she moved against him, riding the pleasure of his touch. She broke the kiss. "Terrence."

"Patience."

Easy for him to say. She was going to go insane with need.

With a quick jerk, he removed her sundress and tossed it on the floor, leaving her in only her panties. She locked gazes with him. His heated stare added fuel to the wildfire running through her.

Dropping to his knees, he tore her underwear off, laced the fingers of one hand with hers, and then lifted one of her legs to drape over his shoulder. Before she could protest, he covered her with his mouth, slipping his tongue into her folds. Her body jerked at first, not expecting the sudden invasion.

Waves of pleasure rolled over her, nipping at her skin. She sank the fingers of her free hand into his hair and squeezed his hand with the other. Terrence licked and sucked while he fingered her. Diana's breaths came in rapid gasps as raw desire built into a climax unlike anything she'd ever had with anyone else.

Still shaking from the orgasm, she was thankful Terrence had cared enough to drag the blanket from the large moon chair and lay it on the floor before easing her down onto it. His dark brown gaze held hers. She smiled at him, pretending they could be like this forever.

You're so beautiful. I'm sorry for being an ass.

She gasped and cupped his face in her hands. Witches were the only ones, besides other shifters, who could mind link with their mates. Her vision blurred as renewed hope for a future filled her heart. *I heard you.*

A brilliant smile formed on his handsome face. "I've opened my heart to you. Even if the curse isn't broken, I'm not leaving. I'll be here in the morning, and the next."

She closed her eyes briefly. *Take the chance, Diana.* "Claim me. Make me yours. Curse be damned!"

A husky chuckle left his lips as he rose to remove his clothes. Nibbling on her bottom lip she said, "Let me help."

With a thought, she stripped him bare and held back a groan at his perfectly sculpted body. A wicked smile curved his lips. "That is a handy little gift."

"I have many talents."

He lowered himself and nipped her ear. "I'm going to enjoy exploring each one."

She opened her mouth to reply, but a groan came out instead as he entered her slowly, stretching her in the best possible way. Bracing her heels against the floor, she raised her hips and met each thrust.

A sharp pain exploded into raw pleasure when he bit her shoulder. His wolf's spirit whispered in her mind as the string of the mating bond wove together, adding to the mounting desire. He increased his thrusts, slamming into her. Every inch of her body was on fire as she fell over the edge and screamed out. The orgasm shook her to the core but intensified when he followed her over the edge with his own release.

Diana snuggled into Terrence as he lay beside her, wrapping his arms and one leg around her. They were connected. She could see the colorful threads of their mating, the bond that connected their souls. Gods, she was mated.

"Terrence?"

"Shh. I just want to hold you right now."

Yeah, that sounded nice. However, her mind was whirling with questions. The main one was whether the curse had broken. It had to have since they were mated. Right?

Terrence let out a heavy sigh. "You're not going to rest until you find out if your grandmother's spell broke too, are you?"

"No. Sorry."

His kissed her forehead. "Let's take a shower and go to the den."

Fear, dread, and glee mingled together in a crazy cocktail of anxiety. She could do it, needed to do it. Her future depended on it. "I'll call Olivia to make sure Grams is there."

If the spell was broken, then her and her sisters were the first generation to fully break their curses. Olivia had mentioned when they were younger that if all three cursed daughters broke their curse, then future generations wouldn't suffer the same fate, and the family was free from the hex.

Please, gods, let that be the case.

CHAPTER FOUR

Terrence gently squeezed Diana's hand. She shook but not out of fear. Nervousness swirled around her. "It'll be okay."

She nodded. "I hope so."

Suddenly, the door to Sawyer and Olivia's home opened. Both of Diana's sisters greeted them with wide smiles. Audrey reached out, grabbed Diana's hand and tugged her inside. "The most amazing thing happened."

Terrence met Sawyer's gaze with a raised brow. Sawyer indicated to one of the armchairs in the living room. Following his gaze, Terrence stilled and stared at the woman sitting quietly as if waiting for Diana. "Who is that?"

"It's their grandmother."

"What?"

Sawyer chuckled and closed the door. "The females will explain."

Watching Diana, Terrence had to force himself to stay put while she stopped in front of her grandmother. She covered her mouth with her hand and her eyes shown with unshed tears. "It worked?"

Grams stood and held out her arms. All three females went to her, wrapping around each other in a group hug. Terrence's chest tightened.

Diana sniffed and asked, "How?"

Grams broke from the hug. "My curse was to age faster and have everyone think I was a crazy old witch. When you found your mate and bound your soul to his, the family's curses were all broken. You girls are free to have children without the fear of them becoming afflicted."

Terrence went to Diana and hugged her tightly. His heart belonged to her, and he'd have it no other way. "I'm really happy for you, but I'm not sure I want kids right now," he whispered in her ear.

She laughed and twisted to face him. "Me either. I want to get to know you and get all of these newly-mated hormones taken care of first."

"Sounds like a plan." He watched how her lavender eyes darkened slightly. He kissed her quickly on the lips. "I'm falling in love with you, even after one night. I know it will only grow and strengthen over the years."

She framed his face, a wide smile on her face. "I've known since the first time I saw you that I could love you."

"Let's sneak over to my place for a quickie."

She pressed her lips together as if holding in a laugh. Her amusement flowed through the mating bond. "A quickie? I think not. My family will understand if we don't come back tonight."

"Then say your goodnights and let's get out of here before I drag you out."

A laugh bubbled out and she slapped at his chest. "Such the animal." She turned to her sisters, who tried not to look like they were listening, then looked back at Terrence. "Take me to my new home."

"Yes, ma'am." He scooped her into his arms and carried her to his, no *their* house where they would spend many decades together.

The End

ABOUT THE AUTHOR

Lia Davis is a mother to two young adults and three equally special kitties, a wife to her soul mate, and a lover of romance. She and her family live in Northeast Florida battling hurricanes and very humid summers. But it's her home and she loves it!

An accounting major, Lia has always been a dreamer with a very active imagination. The wheels in her head never stop. She ventured into the world of writing and publishing in 2008 and loves it more than she imagined. Writing is stress reliever that allows her to go off in her corner of the house and enter into another world that she created, leaving real life where it belongs.

Her favorite things are spending time with family, traveling, reading, writing, chocolate, coffee, nature and hanging out with her kitties.

FIND OUT MORE ABOUT LIA DAVIS HERE:

Website:
http://www.authorliadavis.com

Newsletter:
http://eepurl.com/mBWx5

Facebook:
https://www.facebook.com/lia.davis.52

Facebook Fan Club:
https://www.facebook.com/liadavisfanclub/

Twitter:
@novelbylia